ENERGY EVERYWHERE

LOUD! SOUND ENERGY

Emma Carlson Berne

PowerKiDS press
New York

Published in 2013 by The Rosen Publishing Group, Inc.
29 East 21st Street, New York, NY 10010

First Edition

Editor: Jennifer Way
Book Design: Andrew Povolny

Photo Credits: Cover Aspen Photo/Shutterstock.com; p. 4 Creatas Images/Thinkstock; p. 5 Pierre Verdy/AFP/Getty Images; p. 6 Jupiterimages/Photos.com/Thinkstock; p. 7 Ingram Publishing/Thinkstock; p. 8 Altrendo Images/Stockbyte/Thinkstock; p. 9 (bottom) Hemera/Thinkstock; p. 9 (top) Comstock/Thinkstock; p. 10 Ryan McVay/Digital Vision/Thinkstock; p. 11 U.S. Navy/Getty Images p. 12 Pixland/Thinkstock; p. 13 Jupiterimages/Pixland/Thinkstock; p. 14 Stockbyte/Thinkstock; p. 15 Henry Groskinsky/Time & Life Pictures/Getty Images; p. 16 Justin Lewis/Digital Vision/Getty Images; pp. 17 (left and right), 18, 19, 20 iStockphoto/Thinkstock; p. 21 Kruchankova May/Shutterstock.com; p. 22 Jupiterimages/Polka Dot/Thinkstock.

Library of Congress Cataloging-in-Publication Data

Berne, Emma Carlson.
Loud! : sound energy / by Emma Carlson Berne. — 1st ed.
p.cm. — (Energy everywhere)
Includes index.
ISBN 978-1-4488-9648-6 (library binding) — ISBN 978-1-4488-9754-4 (pbk.) —
ISBN 978-1-4488-9755-1 (6-pack)
1. Sound—Juvenile literature. I. Title.
QC225.5.B475 2013
534—dc23

2012019921

Manufactured in the United States of America

CPSIA Compliance Information: Batch #W13PK4: For Further Information contact Rosen Publishing, New York, New York at 1-800-237-9932

CONTENTS

QUIET OR LOUD: SOUND ENERGY

Whisper in your friend's ear. Now scream at the top of your lungs at a rock concert. Did you know that when you do both of these things, you are letting out sound energy? You make waves of sound when you make any noise at all. In fact, every sound in the world is the result of sound energy.

Quiet sounds, like whispering, produce a small amount of sound energy.

Speaking into a megaphone emits a larger amount of sound energy than does your voice alone.

Energy is the ability of a system to do work, and it comes in many different forms. Light and heat are types of energy. This book will discuss sound energy. It will explain what makes sound, how we hear sound, and how sound is measured.

THE WORLD OF SOUNDS

Close your eyes for a moment after you read this, and think about all the sounds you are hearing right now. Can you hear birds outside? How about the creaking of the chair you are sitting on? If you are very quiet, you may even hear your own breathing.

If everything else around you is very quiet, you might be able to hear the flapping of a bird's wings.

These sounds have different sources. The birds, for instance, are making their own sounds. You are breathing and making the chair creak, though. The world around us is filled with millions of sounds. A pounding jackhammer, a rock band, and the screeching of monkeys in the rain forest are all sources of sound.

Jackhammers produce big sound waves that your whole body can feel if you are nearby.

WHAT ARE SOUND WAVES?

Sounds travel in waves. All sound waves begin with some kind of **vibration** that then travels from the sound's source to your ear. For instance, if you were to tap a glass with a knife, the glass would vibrate. That vibration would cause the air molecules nearby to move back and forth in a wavelike pattern.

If you could see sound waves, they would look as if they had peaks and valleys like waves in the ocean. Loud sounds, like a clap of thunder, have high peaks and deep valleys. Quiet sounds, like the rustle of a leaf, have low peaks and shallow valleys.

Rustling and crunching autumn leaves makes small sound waves even if you jump into a big pile of them!

When you see lightning, count how many seconds pass before you hear thunder. The shorter the time between lightning and thunder, the closer the storm is to where you are.

WHAT IS THUNDER?

Thunder is the sound lightning makes. When a lightning bolt strikes, the air around it becomes super heated. The hot air explodes outward. Just like any other explosion, it creates a loud, booming noise. This is thunder!

If you put your hand in front of a stereo speaker, you can feel the sound waves coming out of it.

THE SPEED OF SOUND

When you ride in an airplane, you are traveling about 600 miles per hour (966 km/h). That is almost as fast as the speed of sound in air, which is about 343 meters per second, or 767 miles per hour (1,235 km/h). Sound must have liquid, solid, or gas matter to travel through. It passes faster through **denser mediums**. This means that sound travels faster through liquids and solids than gases. In a **vacuum**, like outer space, there are no sounds.

Sound can also bounce off of objects. An **echo** is a sound bouncing off of an object.

Sound travels faster through denser mediums. That means sound travels faster through water than it does through air.

WHAT IS A SONIC BOOM?

A sonic boom happens when something travels faster than the speed of sound. If a fighter plane travels faster than sound waves, the air around the plane gets compressed and makes a booming noise.

Here is an airplane as it breaks the sound barrier. The cloudlike formation around the plane is believed to be caused by changes in air pressure created by the plane's speed.

LOUD OR SOFT, HIGH OR LOW

You may have heard of singers being on **pitch**. Pitch refers to whether the sound is low or high. Sounds with low pitch have a low **frequency**. Frequency refers to how fast the particles in a sound wave are vibrating. With a low sound, the particles are vibrating more slowly and the waves in the sound wave are farther apart. Higher-pitched sounds have a higher frequency. The waves in the sound wave are closer together.

The sound of a hammer hitting a nail has high peaks and deep valleys.

A singer who can hit high notes can make sounds with a high frequency.

Volume refers to how loud or soft a sound is. Loud noises have sound waves with high peaks and deep valleys. Softer noises have low peaks and shallow valleys.

AMAZING EARS

Our ears are the organs that allow us to hear sound. The part you can see is the outer ear. Its folds direct sound waves into the ear opening. The sound waves then strike the eardrum, which causes it to vibrate. Three little bones connected to the eardrum send the vibration into the **cochlea**, or inner ear.

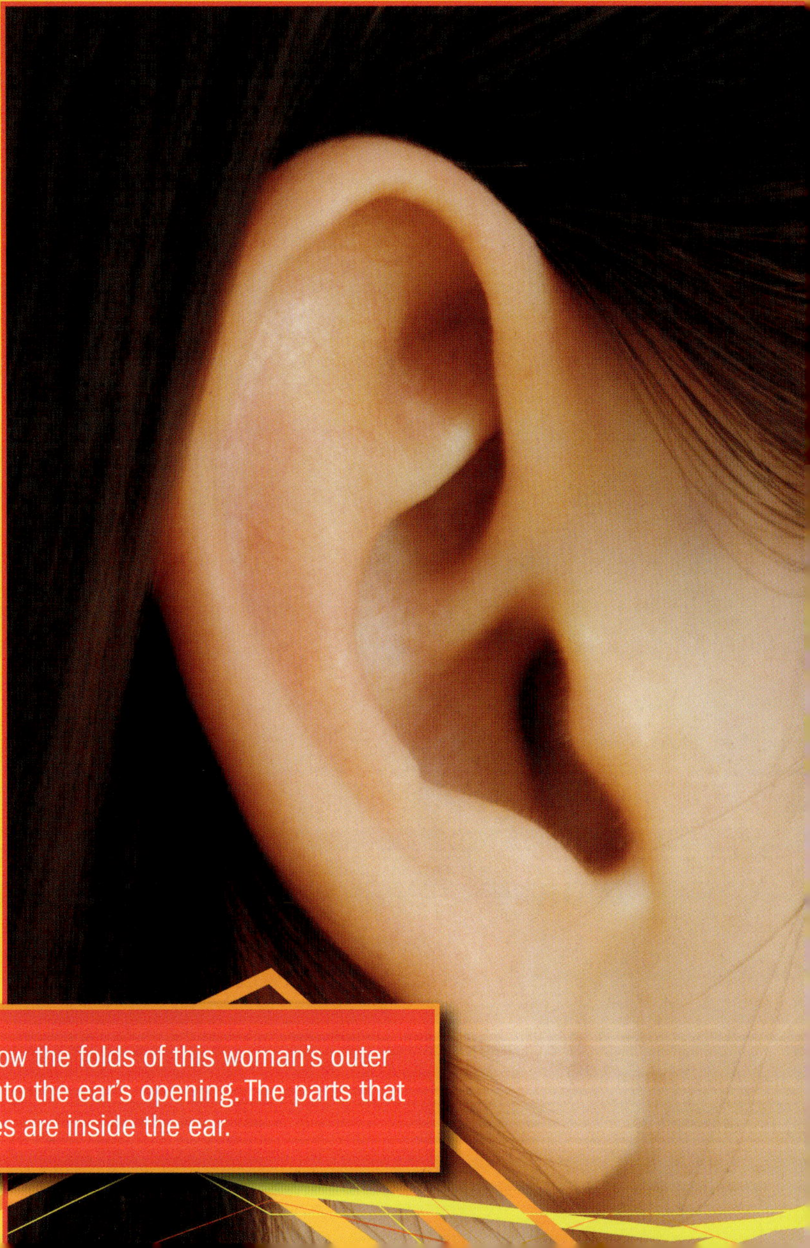

Here you can see how the folds of this woman's outer ear direct sounds into the ear's opening. The parts that pick up sound waves are inside the ear.

Theaters and opera houses, like the one shown here, are designed to make sound bounce around the room in a way that lets everyone in the audience hear a show clearly.

The inner ear has fluid in it, which is set in motion. Tiny hairs connected to the **auditory nerves** then pick up the motion of the fluid. The nerves send signals to the brain. Then the brain puts a meaning to the sound.

SPECIAL SOUNDS

Some sounds are too high-pitched for humans to hear. Animals like dogs, cats, bats, and dolphins can all hear very high sounds that we cannot hear.

Dolphins use echolocation by making clicking sounds. The sounds travel through the water and echo off of objects. This helps dolphins find their way more easily than by sight alone.

Sonar devices like the one shown here are often used for navigation in submarines.

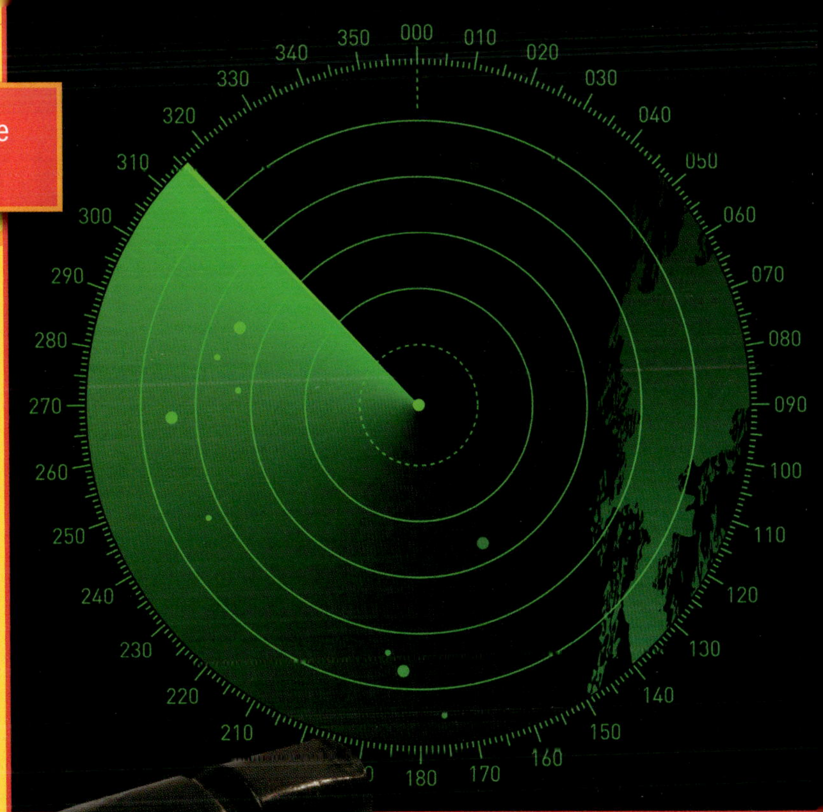

Some animals use sounds to hunt and explore. This is called **echolocation.** Bats and dolphins, for instance, make special noises. When these noises bounce off of objects, the echo tells the animal how close objects are.

This is a dog whistle. It emits a sound that dogs can hear but that is too high-pitched for humans to hear.

A **sonar** device is a machine that makes tiny clicks to measure how far away objects are. The clicks bounce off of objects and are reflected back. The device reads how long the clicks took to come back.

HOW IS SOUND MEASURED?

Sound is measured in a unit called a **decibel**. The **threshold**, or lowest limit of hearing, is 0 decibels. From there, the decibel scale starts going up. Human breathing is about 10 decibels. A vacuum cleaner is 60 decibels. A rocket launch is 140 decibels. After 150 decibels, you can cause damage to your ears and lose your hearing!

An airplane taking off is about 120 decibels.

Here is a sound meter that has a decibel readout. When the needle goes into the red area, the sound is uncomfortably loud.

There are many instruments for measuring sound. One of the most common is a sound meter. The sound meter has a microphone that picks up sound. The meter also has a scale that will show you how many decibels something is.

CHANGING SOUND ENERGY

Energy does not always have to exist in one form. Sound energy, for instance, can be changed into other kinds of energy. Scientists have recently created a kind of battery that can be charged just by absorbing noise. The battery changes sound energy into electrical energy.

The light energy and mechanical energy used to build things in factories also produce sound energy.

Your refrigerator runs on electrical energy. Most of that energy is turned into mechanical energy used to cool and light the inside, but sound energy is produced, too.

Energy cannot be created or destroyed, though. All energy is just converted from some other energy source. When energy is released from a source, it is then used somewhere else.

SOUND AND TECHNOLOGY

The buzz of a bumblebee, the thud of a jackhammer, and the soaring voice of a singer are just some of the millions of sounds that fill our world. Humans have learned to record and control many sounds in our world. For example, every time we talk on the phone or turn on the stereo, we are using technology to listen to sounds that we have harnessed for our own purposes.

When you talk on the phone, the sound waves of your voice are picked up by your phone and transmitted to your friend's phone and into her ear.

GLOSSARY

auditory nerves (AH-dih-tor-ee NERVZ) The nerves that send sound signals to the brain.

cochlea (KO-klee-uh) A snail-shaped tube found in the inner ear.

decibel (DEH-suh-bel) A unit by which sound is measured.

denser (DENTS-er) More closely packed together or thick.

echo (EH-koh) A sound heard again when it bounces off an object.

echolocation (eh-koh-loh-KAY-shun) A method of finding objects by producing a sound and judging the time it takes the echo to return and the direction from which it returns.

frequency (FREE-kwen-see) The number of waves moving in a certain space each second.

mediums (MEE-dee-umz) Things through which forces or effects can pass.

pitch (PICH) How high or low a sound is.

sonar (SOH-nahr) A way of using sound waves to find objects or judge distances.

threshold (THRESH-hohld) The point at which an effect begins.

vacuum (VA-kyoom) A space without air or any other matter.

vibration (vy-BRAY-shun) Fast movement up and down or back and forth.

volume (VOL-yoom) How loud a sound is.

INDEX

WEBSITES

Due to the changing nature of Internet links, PowerKids Press has developed an online list of websites related to the subject of this book. This site is updated regularly. Please use this link to access the list: www.powerkidslinks.com/enev/loud/